Disney
BIG HERO 6

Read-Along
STORYBOOK AND CD

W9-CRA-741

This is the story of how a prodigy named Hiro, an oversized inflatable robot called Baymax, and a group of their friends formed a band of high-tech heroes and saved San Fransokyo. You can read along with me in your book. You'll know it's time to turn the page when you hear this sound. . . .
Let's begin now.

Printed in the United States of America
First Paperback Edition, May 2018
1 3 5 7 9 10 8 6 4 2
Library of Congress Control Number: 2017942201
ISBN 978-1-368-02117-3
FAC-038091-18075

For more Disney Press fun, visit www.disneybooks.com

DISNEY PRESS
Los Angeles • New York

SUSTAINABLE FORESTRY INITIATIVE
Certified Chain of Custody
At Least 20% Certified Forest Content
www.sfiprogram.org
SFI-00993
Logo Applies to Text Stock Only

In an alley in San Fransokyo, a robot battle was about to begin. Mr. Yama, the undefeated champion, was looking for a challenger. Fourteen-year-old genius Hiro Hamada stepped forward with his invention, Megabot. Mr. Yama laughed at Hiro's small robot but agreed to battle. Hiro just smirked as he placed his robot in the ring. "Megabot? Destroy!"

Within minutes, Megabot had wrecked Mr. Yama's robot. Mr. Yama was angry! Luckily, at that moment, Hiro's older brother, Tadashi, rode up on his scooter. Together, the two brothers raced away from Mr. Yama and his goons.

Once they got home, Hiro wanted to go to another bot fight across town. But Tadashi was worried about his little brother. He knew that Hiro could do greater things. "When are you gonna start doing something with that big brain of yours?"

Hiro just shook his head. "What, go to college like you so people can tell me stuff I already know?"

Tadashi was a genius, too. He studied at the San Fransokyo Institute of Technology. He wanted his brother to sign up for classes, but Hiro was not interested. Suddenly, an idea came to Tadashi. He agreed to take Hiro to his bot fight.

Go Go

Wasabi

On the way to the bot fight, Tadashi needed to stop by his lab. There, Hiro met Tadashi's friends Go Go, Wasabi, Honey Lemon, and Fred. They were working on their own inventions. Go Go was using electromagnets to make the fastest bike ever. Wasabi was working on a high-powered laser. And Honey Lemon was formulating a chemical reaction that could turn a big ball of metal into a pile of pink dust!

Hiro was impressed by all of Tadashi's friends and their inventions.

The only one who wasn't a student or an inventor was Fred. He was the school's mascot.

Honey Lemon

Fred

Next Tadashi showed Hiro his own invention—a robot named Baymax who had been programmed to take care of people who were sick or hurt. Tadashi stuck a piece of duct tape on Hiro's arm, and then pulled it off.

"Ow! Hey, hey!" When Hiro yelped, Baymax activated.

"Hello. I am Baymax, your personal health care companion. I was alerted to the need for medical attention when you said 'ow.' On a scale of one to ten, how would you rate your pain?"

Tadashi watched proudly as Baymax scanned Hiro for injuries. "He's gonna help a lot of people."

Hiro was amazed by his brother's invention.

As the brothers were leaving the lab, they ran into Tadashi's teacher Professor Callaghan, a famous scientist. The professor looked at Hiro's bot. "With your bot, winning must come easy."

Hiro shrugged. "Yeah, I guess."

"Well, if you like things easy, then my program isn't for you. We push the boundaries of robotics here. My students go on to shape the future. Good luck with the bot fights."

As soon as Hiro and Tadashi got outside, Hiro turned to his brother. "I *have* to go here. If I don't go to this nerd school, I'm gonna lose my mind!"

Tadashi smiled. His plan had worked!

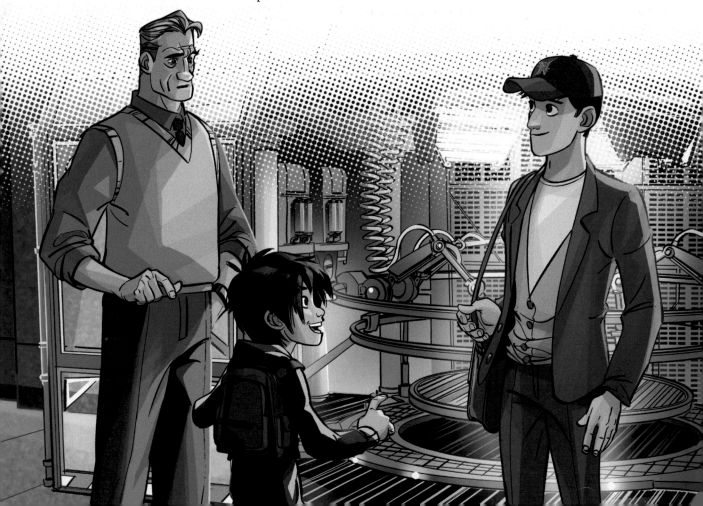

    To get into the San Fransokyo Institute of Technology, Hiro would have to enter an invention in the school's upcoming robotics showcase. If he impressed the judges, he could become a student. Hiro knew he needed to come up with an amazing invention, but he was having trouble thinking of an idea. "I got nothing. I'm done. I'm never getting in."

    Tadashi encouraged his little brother. "Shake things up! Use that big brain of yours to think your way out."

    And then, finally, Hiro came up with a plan. He worked hard to get his project just right.

The night of the showcase arrived. Standing before the crowd, Hiro was nervous but ready to show off his invention. "This is a microbot. It doesn't look like much. But when it links up with the rest of its pals . . . things get a little more interesting."

Hiro tapped the special headband he wore that allowed him to control the tiny robots with his mind. At Hiro's command, the microbots could join together to form any shape or accomplish any task.

"If you can think it, the microbots can do it. The only limit is your imagination!"

The crowd went wild. Everyone loved the microbots! After the showcase, a businessman named Alistair Krei even offered Hiro a lot of money for them. Hiro thought about it, but he turned Krei down. "I appreciate the offer, Mr. Krei. But they're not for sale."

Just then, Professor Callaghan approached Hiro. He was so impressed with Hiro's microbots that he invited Hiro to become a student at the institute. Hiro was very excited.

Outside the showcase hall, Hiro turned to Tadashi. "I wouldn't be here if it wasn't for you, so . . . you know, thanks for not giving up on me."

Just then, people began running from the hall. A fire had broken out, and Professor Callaghan was still inside! Tadashi started to run toward the hall.

"Tadashi! No!" Hiro tried to stop his brother, but it was no use. Tadashi rushed in to find the professor. Moments later, an explosion knocked Hiro to the ground. Tadashi was gone.

As the days passed with Tadashi gone, Hiro stayed in his room and kept to himself. Nothing seemed to matter anymore.

Then, one day, Hiro dropped something on his foot. "Ow! Ah, ow."

To his surprise, Baymax appeared. "Hello. I am Baymax, your personal health care companion. I heard a sound of distress. What seems to be the trouble?"

Hiro didn't want anything to do with Baymax, but Baymax would not turn off. "I cannot deactivate until you say you are satisfied with your care."

As Hiro tried to figure out a way to deactivate Baymax, he noticed something moving under his bed. It was the microbot that had been in his sweatshirt pocket on the night of the showcase. It was moving around, trying to find the other microbots. But all of them had been destroyed in the fire. "This—this doesn't make any sense."

Baymax looked at it. "Your tiny robot is trying to go somewhere."

Hiro shrugged, uninterested. "Oh, yeah? Why don't you, uh, find out where it's trying to go?"

Baymax was programmed to help Hiro, so he followed the microbot. Hiro couldn't let anything happen to his brother's robot. Reluctantly, he took off out the door after him.

Hiro chased Baymax all over San Fransokyo until he finally caught up with the big robot outside an abandoned warehouse.

Baymax turned to Hiro. "I have found where your tiny robot wants to go."

Helping each other, Hiro and Baymax climbed through a window. Once inside, Hiro looked around to find something astonishing. His microbots were there . . . along with a machine that was making thousands more!

Suddenly, the microbots began to assemble. Hiro and Baymax spotted a mysterious man in a mask moving toward them. At the masked man's command, the microbots swarmed together and attacked Hiro and Baymax. Only by thinking quickly were the two able to escape and make their way home.

While Baymax recharged, Hiro thought about what had happened at the warehouse. His microbots hadn't been destroyed in the fire; the masked man had stolen them! And if the masked man was responsible for the fire . . . *"He's responsible for Tadashi."*

Hiro could barely contain his anger. "We gotta catch that guy."

Baymax would do anything to make Hiro feel better. "Will apprehending the man in the mask improve your emotional state?"

Hiro nodded. "If we're gonna catch that guy, you need some upgrades." The big robot wasn't programmed to fight. So Hiro quickly got to work, programming Baymax with new karate moves and building him a special suit of armor. Soon Baymax was battle ready.

To celebrate, Hiro taught Baymax how to fist-bump. "Bah-a-la-la-la!"

Hiro and Baymax returned to
the warehouse. But the microbots
were gone, and the masked man
was nowhere to be found. So the
pair followed Hiro's microbot again,
hoping it would lead them to the
rest of the microbots.

The bot led them to a pier.
Suddenly, through the fog, a wave
of microbots appeared, with the
masked man riding on top of them.

But before Hiro could confront
him, a car pulled up. Baymax had
contacted Go Go, Wasabi, Honey
Lemon, and Fred to help Hiro.

When the mystery man spotted
them, he ordered the microbots to
attack. Just in time, Go Go pulled
Hiro into the car and they drove
away.

The man chased after their car,
riding the swarm of microbots.

Hiro was angry. "Stop the car!
Baymax and I can take this guy!"

But Hiro's friends weren't about
to let anything happen to him.
With Baymax's help, they were able
to escape to safety.

Hiro and his friends went to Fred's house to regroup. They had to figure out who the masked man was. Fred suggested that it might be Alistair Krei. Since Hiro hadn't sold the businessman his microbots, maybe Krei had stolen them instead.

It was possible, but Hiro wanted to be sure. If he upgraded Baymax's programs again, the big robot could scan the whole city until he located the masked man. But Hiro and Baymax wouldn't be able to stop him alone. Hiro looked around at his friends. "Actually, if we're gonna catch this guy, I need to upgrade all of you."

Fred was excited. "You guys, do you feel this? Our origin story begins. We're gonna be superheroes!"

Hiro created a unique super suit for each of his friends. Go Go's suit had electromagnetic wheels like her bike's, allowing her to speed around and throw disks from her wrists. Honey Lemon's suit came with a purse that contained a portable chemistry lab. Wasabi's had gloves with lasers in them that could slice through anything. And Fred's suit made him look like a monster. When he was wearing it, he could jump really high and breathe fire!

Baymax's new armor had a rocket fist and wings. And thanks to the magnets Hiro had sewn into his own suit, he would be able to ride through the air stuck to Baymax's back.

The team practiced using their new suits. Then they came up with a game plan; the villain's mask controlled the microbots, so taking it away was the only way they could stop him.

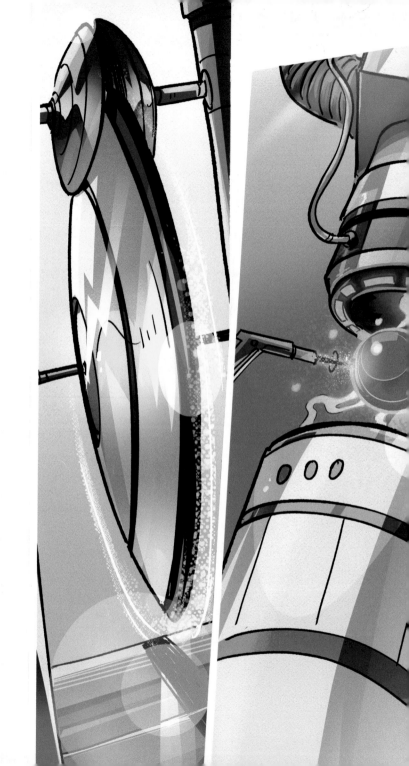

Later that day, Hiro climbed on Baymax's back for their first big flight. The ride was a little bumpy at the beginning, but soon Baymax was soaring through the air like a pro. Hiro was thrilled. "Yes! Woo-hoo!"

"The treatment is working."

On their initial flight, Baymax used his scanner to detect the masked man. He was located on an island called Akuma across the bay. Later that day, the group flew to Akuma, where they found an abandoned lab formerly owned by Alistair Krei. As the team looked around, they activated video footage of an experiment led by Krei. The footage showed a young pilot named Abigail being sent in a pod through a teleportation portal. But the experiment went wrong and the portal exploded! The team was stunned. The masked man had to be Krei. Just then, the masked man attacked them!

3:21:46

Using their new suits, the team attempted to fight back. In the chaos, Hiro managed to pull off the man's mask. It was Professor Callaghan!

Hiro was confused. "But the explosion . . . you died."

"No, I had your microbots." The professor explained how he had used the microbots to protect himself.

Furious that the professor hadn't helped his brother, Hiro ordered Baymax to attack Callaghan. "Baymax, destroy!"

Baymax shook his head. "My programming prevents me from injuring a human being."

"Not anymore!" In a rage, Hiro ripped out the green nurse chip Tadashi had put into Baymax's chest. Baymax pointed his rocket fist at Callaghan and tried to blast him. But Hiro's friends stopped the big robot, allowing Callaghan to escape.

Angry and frustrated, Hiro flew off on Baymax.

Back at home, Hiro wanted to go after Callaghan and get revenge. But Baymax didn't want to hurt anyone; that was not why Tadashi had created him. He showed Hiro a video of his brother. "Tadashi is here."

The video showed Tadashi trying again and again to get Baymax to activate. When he finally did, Tadashi was overjoyed. "You're gonna help so many people, buddy. So many."

As Hiro watched the video, his anger began to fade. Tadashi had wanted to help people, not hurt them. He would have been disappointed if Hiro used his invention to harm someone.

Just then, Hiro's friends arrived with something Hiro needed to see. Go Go played video footage that showed Callaghan yelling at Krei after the failed portal experiment. They flipped through to the end of the video and they saw Callaghan saying good-bye to Abigail, the pilot . . . who was his daughter! Callaghan wanted to use the microbots to punish Krei for the loss of his daughter.

Fred was shocked. "This is a revenge story."

Hiro looked at his friends. "So what are we waiting for?"

The group rushed to Krei's new company headquarters to find him addressing an audience. Suddenly, Callaghan appeared. "You took everything from me when you sent Abigail into that machine. Now I'm taking everything from you!"

At Callaghan's command, the microbots reassembled the remaining parts of the portal from the lab. Krei's new building started to get sucked into the open portal. Somehow Hiro and the team had to stop Callaghan. Then Hiro got an idea. "Go for the mask!"

Without it, Callaghan wouldn't be able to control the microbots.

Together, the team tried to stop Callaghan, but he was too strong. Hiro realized they needed a new plan. "Forget the mask. Take out the bots! They'll get sucked up into the portal!"

Using their super suits, the team chipped away at the columns of microbots. One by one, the bots got sucked into the portal. And without them, Callaghan was finally defeated.

But the danger wasn't over yet. The portal was still open. It started to break apart. Hiro had to get his friends to safety. "We need to get out of here now!"

The team turned to run when, suddenly, Baymax noticed something. He pointed at the portal. "My sensor is detecting signs of life—coming from there."

It was Callaghan's daughter. She was still alive! Hiro jumped onto Baymax's back and they flew into the portal to save Abigail.

Dodging the swirling debris, they sped through the vortex until they found her still in her pod, unconscious.

Hiro grabbed Abigail's pod, but suddenly, a large chunk of concrete hit Baymax, damaging his armor.

Without it, Baymax couldn't fly. But he could still save Hiro and Abigail by using his rocket fist to propel them through the portal before it closed. He turned to Hiro. "I cannot deactivate until you say you are satisfied with your care."

Hiro shook his head. "Please. No. I can't lose you, too."

"Hiro, I will always be with you."

Tearfully, Hiro hugged his best friend good-bye. "I'm satisfied with my care."

With that, Baymax detached from his rocket fist and drifted away.

Thanks to Baymax, Hiro and Abigail made it back through the portal just in time. Hiro and his friends had saved the day. Abigail was safe. Callaghan went to jail.

And Hiro finally became a student at the San Fransokyo Institute of Technology, just like Tadashi had hoped. He even got to use Tadashi's old lab space.

As Hiro unpacked his things, he placed Baymax's rocket fist on his desk. Smiling sadly, Hiro gave it a fist bump.

"Bah-a-la-la-la." The robot fist uncurled. That was when Hiro spotted Baymax's green nurse chip.

In no time, Hiro had rebuilt Baymax. "I am Baymax, your personal health care companion. Hello, Hiro."

Hiro, Go Go, Wasabi, Honey Lemon, Fred, and Baymax were heroes. If another danger ever threatened San Fransokyo, they would be ready.

"We didn't set out to be superheroes. But sometimes life doesn't go the way you planned. The good thing is my brother wanted to help a lot of people. And that's what we're gonna do. Who are we?"

They were the Big Hero 6!